squid. That's a funny word. squid.

My new X ray goggles allow me to see bones.

Chilly, I hope you know your machines are never going to work. Everybody knows it. but you. JUST GIVE UP.

—Vinnie

Vinnie

p.s. I threw your lunchbox in the deep waters.
ha ha ha ha ha ha ha ha

For Isaac: always think beyond your iceberg.
My goal is to make you proud of me.—J.R.

J. RUTLAND writes and illustrates picture books and graphic novels at his home
in Asheville, North Carolina. He lives there with his wife, son, daughter, and black dog.
This is his first invention for NorthSouth Books.
Subscribe: patreon.com/escapistcomix
Custom work: jrutlandcustoms.com/
Instagram: @jrutlandart

———————————————————————

Text and illustrations copyright © 2018 by Jarrett Rutland.
First published in the United States, Great Britain, Canada, Australia, and New Zealand in 2018
by NorthSouth Books, Inc., an imprint of NordSüd Verlag AG, CH-8050 Zürich, Switzerland.
First paperback edition 2020.

Distributed in the United States by NorthSouth Books, Inc., New York 10016.
Library of Congress Cataloging-in-Publication Data is available.
ISBN: 978-0-7358-4283-0 (trade)
ISBN: 978-0-7358-4422-3 (PB)
Printed in China, 2020.
3 5 7 9 11 · 10 8 6 4 2
www.northsouth.com

MIX
Paper from
responsible sources
FSC® C144853
FSC
www.fsc.org

CHILLY DA VINCI

J. RUTLAND

North
South

My name is Chilly, and while others do "penguin" things, I build machines.

Unfortunately, they don't always work.

My flying machine, the *Good Bird*, cracked the ice. Now we're drifting away from Vinci, the colony's glacier, on a small iceberg. And Vinnie won't stop gakkering at me.

NOTE: It's official. My flying machines stink like rotten orca blubber in the midday sun.

sploosh

After the Big Crack Setback, a large orca has found us, like crumbs on a floating plate. It is taking bites out of the iceberg. I swear I heard it giggle.

The others agreed when Vinnie said I was "not good at being a penguin." They'll change their minds when my new machine gets us back to Vinci.

First, I'll draw up my plans.... I'll use sea junk, and build the *Polar Roller*, which will skim across the water in style!

metal panels (20)

It sank like a stone! What was I thinking?
One cannot simply drive across the water.
My brain is full of seawater, and my
sketchbook is full of goof-ups.

Did I mention it wouldn't move anyway
if it had to drag Mr. Plumpy Fin? Luckily
all the penguins made it out safely.

With the ka-chunk of
the pulleys ... I won't
hear Vinnie shouting insults.
Why does he feel the need
to throw sea junk at me?
He's wasting supplies.

That won't stop me. Great
inventors never give up.

15

Back on
Vinci

Chilly's my hero.

Will you sign my
flipper?

The orca didn't give up either.

NOTE: I am terrible at thinking. I should do it less. How can I, a tiny gathering of flightless feathers, move an iceberg? My pulleys didn't pulley. My engine didn't engine.

Boy, Plumpy Fin really likes splashes. If I were to look at the bite—I mean the bright—side, I have been in the air a lot longer than on the *Good Bird*.

In recovery time I made night vision goggles, but everything looks green. The ladies who chick-sit me made me kelp casserole. (I don't eat fish.)

I hope it's not my last supper.

What kind of penguin doesn't eat fish?

Mr. Plumpy Fin has eaten most of the iceberg. We're running out of time. I wish I was a seagull, just using the wind to drift around and look at stars.... Wait! *Wind!*

I've got it! I'll revisit something that did not work before: a flying machine.

I'll use leather for the wings so they won't tear. And I'll use bones. They're light but still strong. If it works, it will carry everyone home to Vinci.

I've logged a ton of drawings of seagull wings acting as sails.

A little rope there, a pulley here, and ... the *Great Bird* is ready!

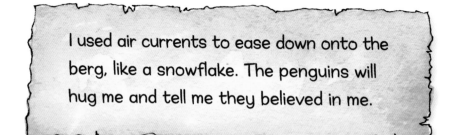

I used air currents to ease down onto the berg, like a snowflake. The penguins will hug me and tell me they believed in me.

Um... guys

No time for hugs! The iceberg is shrinking, and Plumpy Fin is circling.

Ticket please.
Vinnie, you're seat 5A.
Just in time! Plumpy Fin has eaten the crust off the berg and is preparing for the center. Plumpy is ready for the main course.
NOTE: more ladders next time.

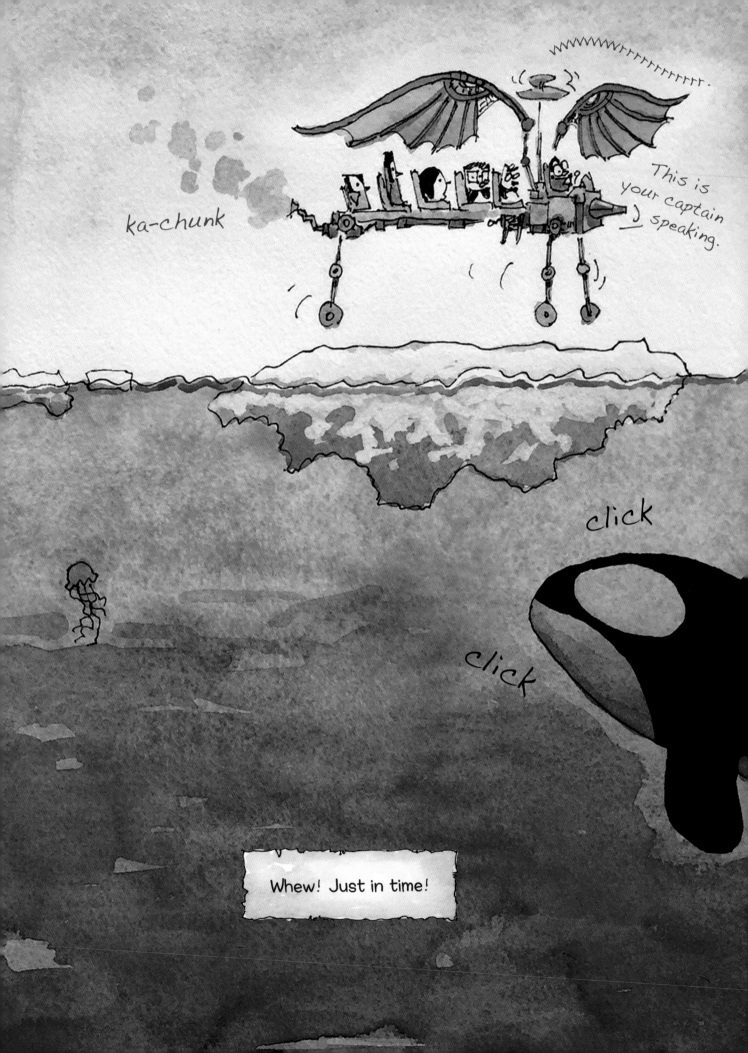

The landing went fine.
A little snow up the beak
never hurt anyone.

WHOOSH!!

We made it at last!
As soon as we stopped,
penguins rushed to greet us.

GAKKER

It's good to finally be back on Vinci. Penguins are reunited. The kelp is in good supply.

Looking back, it was an exciting adventure.

PARTY PARTY

PARTY

My flippers are in one piece. I don't have to hear Vinnie gakker at me all the time, and everyone is safely back at the colony away from Plumpy Fin.

barnacle.

bar-nackle.

good

Author's Note

Chilly da Vinci was partially inspired by Leonardo da Vinci, a human (not a penguin) who lived in Italy during the fifteenth century—more than five hundred years ago.

Leonardo was known as the original "Renaissance Man" since he was remarkably talented in so many areas. He's best known for his paintings Mona Lisa and The Last Supper, as well as for his scientific endeavors. His endless research, along with his relentless need for his ideas to work, made him an innovator whose work is still studied today.

Indeed, Leonardo was very talented, but among his successes, many of his contraptions were failures. Even though he had more designs than were able to be counted, we only know of one early glider he constructed, which was unsuccessful. Yet by actually using Leonardo's blueprints to build his other hang gliders (which were a combination of stationary and man-powered mechanical wings), scientists have proven that his later designs will fly.

The inspiring stories of both Leonardo and Chilly are reminders to focus on the process, not the reward. That's an important lesson to remember when dealing with a reward you desperately want. And, often, you may find the solution lies not in scrapping your work, but merely in something that's been accessible all along—something you can study from a different angle and then revise.

Go forth, young innovators, and be masters of your iceberg!

jellyfish

jellyfish

jellyfish